The Story of CHRISTMAS

The Story of CHRISTMAS

Baby Jesus Is Born
The Visit of the Wise Men
Simeon and the Baby Jesus

An ARCH BOOKS® Gift Collection

*An Inspirational Press Book
for Children*

C
Sto

First Inspirational Press edition published in 1998.

Inspirational Press
A division of BBS Publishing Corporation
386 Park Avenue South
New York, NY 10016

Inspirational Press is a registered trademark of BBS Publishing Corporation.

Published by arrangement with Arch® Books, a division of Concordia
Publishing House, 3558 S. Jefferson Avenue, St. Louis, Missouri 63118-3968.

Library of Congress Catalog Card Number: 98-72400

ISBN: 0-88486-211-9

Printed in Mexico.

Baby Jesus Is Born

Luke 2:1–20 for Children
Written by Gloria A. Truitt
Illustrated by Kathy Mitter

There was a Roman emperor
    Two thousand years ago,
Who asked the folks he ruled to make
    A trip quite hard and slow.

All people had to travel to
    The town from where they came.
(So they could all be counted, each
    Was asked to sign his name.)

Now in the town of Nazareth—
    In the land of Galilee—
There lived a man named Joseph and
    His promised wife-to-be.

Mary was the woman's name.
She was God's *favored one,*
For God had chosen her to be
The mother of His Son.

Joseph knew he had to heed
The emperor's decree,
So he and Mary set out from
The land of Galilee.

At last they came to Bethlehem,
A town of little size.
Now the streets were crowded, which
Was not a great surprise!

Quickly Joseph found an inn,
　　The only one in town,
For Mary was exhausted and
　　She needed to lie down.

Joseph asked the innkeeper,
　　"Do you have room for two?"
"No," he said to Joseph, who
　　Then sighed, "What should I do?"

"I'm sorry," said the innkeeper,
  "I really am unable
To provide a room for you . . .
  But wait! I have a stable!"

Joseph looked at Mary, then
  He sadly shook his head.
"At least you will be safe from harm,
  And you can rest," he said.

Now, on that night our Lord was born
To save all folk on earth,
And that is why we still today
Observe His holy birth!

This baby was the promised King—
        God's Son, this couple knew—
And so they named Him Jesus,
        As God had told them to.

Some shepherds in a field nearby
Were tending to their flock,
When suddenly an angel came!
Imagine their great shock!

God's holy light surrounded them,
And they were so dismayed!
But then the angel of the Lord
Said, "Do not be afraid!

"I bring you good and joyous news
For everyone this day!
A Savior has been born to you!
To Him, go find your way.

"You'll find this baby wrapped in cloths
And lying in a manger.
You'll know Him by these signs and, so,
This Child won't be a stranger."

Then suddenly great numbers of
God's angels from the sky
Appeared and sang His praises,
"Glory be to God on high!"

The shepherds said to one another,
"Could this really be?
Our Savior born in Bethlehem?
Quick! Let's go and see!"

They hurried off and found the Child,
Just as the angel said,
Inside a humble stable with
A manger for His bed.

They knelt beside this holy Child,
　　Then ran to spread the word,
Telling everyone they met
　　Of what they'd seen and heard!

Dear Parents:

Take a minute with your child during the busy Christmas season to worship the Christ Child, born to be your Savior. After reading this story, act it out, using the figures from your crèche set. Assure your child of Jesus' great love—so great that He willingly exchanged His heavenly throne for a bed of straw and a cross.

Read the last page to your child again, explaining that the shepherds did not keep the good news of Jesus' birth to themselves. Invite friends or neighbors to your home for a Christmas devotion. Share with everyone around you the message that Jesus was born to be our Savior.

The Editor

The Visit of the Wise Men

Matthew 2:1–12

Written by Martha Streufert Jander

Illustrated by Robert Cassell

Long ago and far away
    some thinkers—very wise—
Each evening watched the sun go down;
    they watched the starry skies.

They knew the moon; they knew each star;
    they studied planets, too.
The Wise Men drew their charts and maps;
    their wisdom grew and grew.

One night as darkness dimmed the light
and stars began to shine,
Appeared a brand-new star to them—
a star so big, so fine.

The Wise Men knew a special joy;
they shouted out, "Prepare!
This star can only mean one thing:
A King is born! But where?"

They left their homes to find that King;
    they carried gifts of love.
The star shone brightly on their way,
    a brilliant guide above.

'Twas Jesus whom they rightly sought;
    'twas Herod whom they found—
The king of all Jerusalem,
    the meanest man around.

The Wise Men asked King Herod, "Where,
    oh, where's this newborn King?
We want to worship Him with love,
    to Him our praises sing."

But evil Herod couldn't say
    where Jesus had been born.
He did not know, he could not tell
    what happened Christmas morn.

So Herod told his scholars, "You
    must look for all you're worth
In ev'ry book and scroll to learn
    this place of kingly birth."

They answered, "Yes! In Bethlehem,
    King David's family town—
That must be where this Babe lives now."
    (King Herod hid his frown.)

That awful king paced back and forth;
    he was a jealous man!
"Another king will take my crown,"
    he thought. Then made a plan:

"Please go and find this King," he said,

"then hurry back and say
Exactly where He lives so I
can worship Him some d[ay]"

King Herod's very wicked heart
had blurted out this lie.
He'd never worship Jesus Christ;
he wanted Him to die!

The Wise Men left Jerusalem
to go to Bethlehem,
And in the darkened sky they saw
the star, still guiding them.

So they rejoiced with happy hearts;
with hope they traveled fast
Until they saw the star stand still.
They'd found the Babe at last!

In front of Jesus, bowing down,
   they praised their Savior-Lord.
With gifts of gold and frankincense
   and myrrh He was adored.

But in a dream that night they heard
the voice of God say, "Go,
Returning home another way,
but not to Herod! No!"

The Wise Men did what God had said,
   though Herod's anger flew;
For Jesus, Savior, Son of God,
   had godly work to do.

DEAR PARENTS:

The Wise Men—not members of God's people and living far away—would seem to be unlikely worshipers of the Christ Child. And yet, so eager were they to worship Him and bring Him gifts that they overcame countless difficulties, including the treachery of the king who ruled in the very city where God's temple stood.

It would be a beautiful thing if we could catch more of that enthusiasm for worship and gift-bringing—and communicate it to our children. Our knowledge of what God in His overwhelming love has done for us in sending His Son into the world—reconciling sinful humanity to Himself through Jesus' atoning death—is so much greater than that of the Wise Men. And we certainly don't have to overcome the kind of obstacles they faced!

It has been said: "Wise men seek Him still." God grant us—and our children—such heavenly wisdom!

THE EDITOR

SIMEON and the BABY JESUS

Luke 2:21-32 for children

Written by Evelyn Marxhausen
Illustrated by
Susan Stochr Morris

One morning in Jerusalem
    The sun began to rise
As kindly, aged Simeon
    Awoke and rubbed his eyes.

He got right out of bed and thought
    This just might be the day
He'd hear some news about the Savior;
    So . . . he knelt to pray.

"Dear God, because I'm old, I pray
    Don't let me die until
Mine eyes have seen the glory of
    Your people Israel."

God promised kind old Simeon
    He'd live to see the day
When Christ, the Savior, would be born
    To take our sins away.

So each day Simeon would pray
    The promise would come true,
Believing God with all his heart
    And trusting in Him, too.

Though Simeon was getting old
    (His face was really wrinkled),
When picturing his Savior's birth
    His brown eyes simply twinkled.

And then it really happened there
In Bethlehem one night.
When everything was quiet, still,
A star shone very bright.

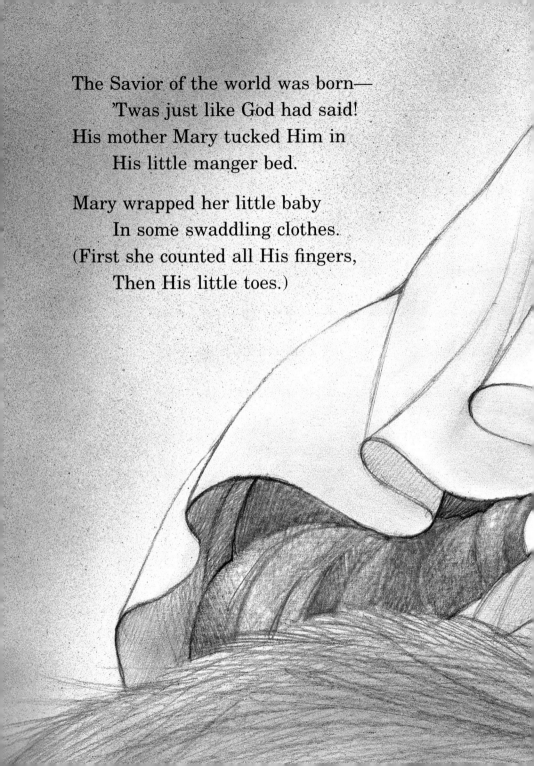

The Savior of the world was born—
    'Twas just like God had said!
His mother Mary tucked Him in
    His little manger bed.

Mary wrapped her little baby
    In some swaddling clothes.
(First she counted all His fingers,
    Then His little toes.)

Joseph stroked the donkey's back;
It brought them all the way
From Nazareth to Bethlehem;
It never went astray.

The animals were happy, too.
    The cows were softly "mooing."
The donkey brayed; the sheep said, "Baa";
    The doves began their cooing.

Nearby the sky was filled with angels
 Singing "Peace on Earth!"
They told some lowly shepherds there
 About the Savior's birth

The shepherds ran to Bethlehem;
 They didn't waste a minute.
When they found the manger bed,
 The tiny babe was in it!

The shepherds, then, told everyone;
The people were amazed.
When Simeon had heard the news,
He shouted, "God be praised!"

Then to the temple Simeon
    Set forth with flying hair.
For God had told him, "If you wait,
    You'll see the baby there."

And after many days had passed
    The happy couple came.
A priest looked at the baby boy
    And said, "Announce His name."

The mother looked so tenderly
    Upon her tiny child,
"It's Jesus," she then whispered low;
    And Joseph proudly smiled.

When Mary's little baby was
    Presented to the Lord;
She offered up two turtledoves—
    'Twas all she could afford.

Then Simeon beheld the babe.
And, moved by God's great love,
He took the baby in his arms
And praised the Lord above.

"Now I can die in peace," he said,
"My soul will be at rest;
Mine eyes have seen the Savior—now
The whole world will be blessed."

DEAR PARENTS:

No matter from which perspective the Christmas story is told, the radiance of its message never diminishes: "for God so loved the world that he gave his one and only Son, that whoever believes in him shall not perish but have eternal life" (John 3:16 NIV).

This gift of a son is why the angels rejoiced and praised their Creator that first Christmas, singing, "Glory to God in the highest, and on earth peace to men on whom his favor rests." This perfect Gift is also the reason the shepherds, after they had seen the Christ Child, "spread the word concerning what had been told them about this child."

We should not wonder then why Simeon, who was "waiting for the consolation of Israel," uttered in the temple that day the prayer of thanks we now know as the Nunc Dimittis, for now he had seen for himself God's marvelous Gift to His children: "a light for revelation to the gentiles and for the glory of [God's] people Israel."

Teach your child that, just as Simeon trusted God's promise to him, so also we can trust that our heavenly Father will not abandon us or let us down. God's promises are sure, and He welcomes us home with the warm outstretched arms of a loving father.

THE EDITOR